Singing with Momma Lou

by LINDA JACOBS ALTMAN

illustrations by **LARRY JOHNSON**

Lee & Low Books Inc. • New York

Text copyright © 2002 by Linda Jacobs Altman
Illustrations copyright © 2002 by Larry Johnson
All rights reserved. No parts of the contents of this book may be reproduced
by any means without written permission of the publisher.
LEE & LOW BOOKS Inc., 95 Madison Avenue, New York, NY 10016
www.leeandlow.com

Printed in China

Book design by Tania Garcia
Book production by The Kids at Our House

The text is set in Adobe Garamound
The illustrations are rendered in acrylic

10 9 8 7 6 5 4 3 2 1
First Edition

Library of Congress Cataloging-in-Publication Data
Altman, Linda Jacobs.
        Singing with Momma Lou / written by Linda Jacobs Altman ; illustrated by Larry Johnson.— 1st ed.
            p. cm.
        Summary: Nine-year-old Tamika uses photographs, school yearbooks, movie ticket stubs,
and other mementos to try to restore the memory of her grandmother, who has Alzheimer's disease.
        ISBN 1-58430-040-X
        [1. Alzheimer's disease—Fiction. 2. Grandmothers—Fiction. 3. African Americans—Fiction.]
    I. Johnson, Larry, 1949- ill. II. Title.
    PZ7.A46393 Si 2002
    [Fic]—dc21   2001029721

In Memory: Elizabeth Zachary, Ethel Altman
—L.J.A.

To my granddaughter, Brooke, who helps me
see my past and future in her eyes —L.J.

It was Sunday again, and raining. The sky was as gray as Tamika's mood. She peered out the car window and sighed. "I still don't see why we have to do this every week. Half the time Momma Lou doesn't even know who we are."

"But the other half of the time she does," said Tamika's father.

"And that," her mother added, "is reason enough."

Tamika knew there was no use arguing. Other families watched football on Sunday afternoons, or had cookouts in the backyard. The Jordans went to the nursing home. That had been the way of things for almost two years.

Momma Lou had something called Alzheimer's disease. Tamika didn't know much about it except that it made Momma Lou forget things.

As usual, the old woman was sitting in the community room, clasping and unclasping her gnarled hands and singing to herself. Momma Lou sang all the time: hymns and spirituals, blues and soul, and once in a while old TV commercials.

"Go say hello," Tamika's father whispered, and nudged her in Momma Lou's direction.

Tamika bit her lip. She used to tell her dreams and deepest secrets to Momma Lou. Now she had to tell her name. "I'm Tamika Louella Jordan, Momma Lou," she said. "I was named after you. I'm nine years old . . . almost ten."

Momma Lou looked Tamika up and down, as if she were seeing her for the first time. "You're skinny as a stick, child. Folks not feeding you?" The old woman didn't wait for an answer. She threw back her head and started to sing:

"They call me skinny, but I'm really just doggone tall . . ."

Everyone in the community room turned to stare. Tamika wished she could scoot under a sofa and hide. Her parents just laughed.

"That's 'Skinny Blues,'" said Momma Lou. "Wrote it myself, back in my singin' days."

Momma Lou smiled then. But just with her mouth, not with her eyes. Her eyes were empty. She started telling Tamika's parents how she spent yesterday at a civil rights rally, listening to Martin Luther King give a speech. The Jordans never reminded her that Dr. King had been dead for years.

Tamika turned away. While the grown-ups talked, she found herself a corner and stayed there. When her parents said it was time to leave, she darted out of the room without a word of good-bye.

Her parents didn't like that one bit. Tamika could tell by their silence on the drive home.

That night after supper Tamika's father took out Momma Lou's scrapbooks. There were pictures of Momma Lou singing with bands and choirs, marching in civil rights demonstrations, dressed for her wedding in an African bridal robe. There was even a newspaper clipping of Momma Lou in jail with a crowd of protestors, all of them singing "We Shall Overcome."

The last pictures Tamika saw that night reminded her of the days of secrets and dreams, when Momma Lou was her best friend in all the world. There was Momma Lou reading her bedtime stories, teaching her to ride a bike, and dressing her like an angel for her first ever Christmas pageant.

"My halo kept slipping," said Tamika, smiling with the memory.

Her father laughed. Then he held up a picture of Momma Lou smiling tenderly into the face of a newborn baby.

"You were her first grandchild. She loved you like nothing I've seen. Now, I figure that's worth a few Sunday afternoons, memory or no memory. Don't you?"

"Yes, Daddy," Tamika said quietly.

Then and there Tamika decided to do something that was supposed to be impossible: give Momma Lou back her memories. Not all of them maybe, but some. There had to be a way to give back at least some.

Tamika started the very next week, with the grandbaby picture.
All the way to the nursing home she practiced what she was going to
do and say. When she got there, she walked right up to Momma Lou,
hugged her, and said, "I'm Tamika Louella Jordan, Momma Lou. I
was named after you. I'm nine years old . . . almost ten."

She handed Momma Lou the picture. "This is us . . . you and me."

Momma Lou looked hard at Tamika, then at the picture in her
hand. "This little baby's you?"

"That's me."

Momma Lou smiled. "Well, you surely have grown," she said, and
a hint of memory twinkled in her eyes for a moment.

Tamika wanted to cheer. It worked! She had reached something in her grandmother, something deep down that not even Alzheimer's had touched.

Momma Lou held the picture against her and closed her eyes. Softly she began to sing, "Rock-a-bye, baby, in the treetop . . ."

Tamika joined her. "When the wind blows, the cradle will rock." It was a special time.

With every visit Tamika brought another memento from Momma Lou's past. There were school yearbooks and pressed corsages, autograph books with fake leather covers, ticket stubs from movies and concerts long past.

Tamika learned the story to go with each memento and told it to her grandmother. They sang songs together, making up new words when it suited them.

And so it went. Autumn turned to winter and finally to spring again. Nine-almost-ten became plain old ten.

Momma Lou got worse. Sometimes she didn't recognize the mementos Tamika brought her. Sometimes she hardly spoke at all.

When she stopped singing, even Tamika's parents got discouraged.

Tamika wouldn't quit. She went through Momma Lou's things three times.

She thought and thought. What could reach through the darkness that had settled over her grandmother's mind? Finally she found the perfect thing—the newspaper story about civil rights demonstrators getting arrested.

The next Sunday Tamika took the clipping with her to the nursing home. She found Momma Lou sitting in a rocking chair staring at an empty wall.

"Hello, Momma Lou," she said. "I'm Tamika Louella Jordan, and I was named after you. I'm ten years old."

Tamika unfolded the clipping and pointed to the picture. "Look, Momma Lou. This is you in jail."

Momma Lou looked, then looked again. "Well, now . . . the klink, the joint, the Calaboose . . . My secret life of crime."

She laughed then a deep booming sound that started in her chest and rolled in great waves from her lips. The laugh was infectious. Tamika caught it and laughed until she almost cried. Her parents caught it too.

They were all busy laughing when Momma Lou closed
her eyes and began to sway. Her voice rose over the laughter
she had started and turned it into a prayer.

She sang "We Shall Overcome" the way it must have
sounded that day in the jailhouse: deep and rich and free.

Tamika joined her grandmother, and together they sang. Soon other voices picked up the song until half the people in the sitting room were singing, swaying together, sharing the moment.

When the singing finished, Momma Lou pressed
the clipping into Tamika's hand. "Don't let this get
lost, honey," she whispered.

Tamika saw the tears in her grandmother's eyes
and knew—this wasn't about one yellowed
newspaper clipping. It was about the memories
Momma Lou was losing. It was about her whole life.

"Don't you worry, Momma Lou," said Tamika.
"I'll keep it safe."

That was the last time Tamika really talked with
her grandmother. Momma Lou's eyes went empty
and stayed that way. It was sad of course, and
Tamika cried. But mostly she remembered.

Tamika made a special scrapbook of all the things she had shared with Momma Lou. She looked at it every now and then. And sometimes when she was scared or uncertain or just plain blue, she would close her eyes and sing "We Shall Overcome" until the world seemed a brighter and a better place.

Alzheimer's disease is an age-related disorder that currently affects approximately four million Americans. It is one of the most widespread diseases among the elderly. Alzheimer's affects the memory centers of the brain, destroying healthy cells. As the cells die, memories fade and disappear.

Initially Alzheimer's sufferers may get easily confused or have difficulty thinking clearly. Later on they may forget how to do the simplest tasks, like dressing themselves or answering the telephone. Eventually they do not recognize even their closest relatives and friends.

Today there is no known cure for Alzheimer's disease, but scientists are working hard to find one.

◆　◆　◆　◆

More information about Alzheimer's disease is available from the following organizations.

Alzheimer's Association
919 North Michigan Avenue, Suite 1100
Chicago, Illinois 60611-1676
Phone: 800-272-3900
Web site: www.alz.org

**Alzheimer's Disease Education
and Referral (ADEAR) Center**
P.O. Box 8250
Silver Spring, MD 20907-8250
Phone: 800-438-4380
Web site: www.alzheimers.org

The Alzheimer's Disease Core Center (ADCC)
320 East Superior Street, Searle 11-450,
Chicago, Illinois 60611-3008
Phone: 312-908-9339
Web site: www.brain.nwu.edu/core/index.htm